Poppleton
AND FRIENDS

Read more
Poppleton
books!

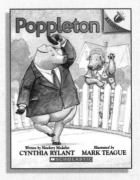

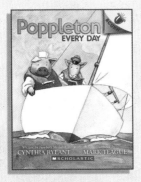

Poppleton
AND FRIENDS

Written by Newbery Medalist
CYNTHIA RYLANT

Illustrated by
MARK TEAGUE

ACORN™
SCHOLASTIC INC.

Library of Congress Cataloging-in-Publication Data

Names: Rylant, Cynthia, author. | Teague, Mark, illustrator. | Rylant, Cynthia. Poppleton ; 2. Title: Poppleton and friends / written by Newbery Medalist Cynthia Rylant ; illustrated by Mark Teague. Description: [New edition] | New York : Acorn/Scholastic Inc., [2019] | Series: Poppleton ; 2 | Originally published: New York : Blue Sky Press, 1997. | Summary: Poppleton the pig goes to the beach, solves a dry skin mystery, and learns that friends are the secret to a long life.
Identifiers: LCCN 2018055821 | ISBN 9781338566697 (pb) | ISBN 9781338566703 (hc) | ISBN 9781338566802 (ebk)
Subjects: LCSH: Poppleton (Fictitious character) — Juvenile fiction. | Swine — Juvenile fiction. | Friendship — Juvenile fiction. | Beaches — Juvenile fiction. | CYAC: Pigs — Fiction. | Friendship — Fiction. | Beaches — Fiction.
Classification: LCC PZ7.R982 Pr 2019 | DDC 813.54 [E] — dc23
LC record available at https://lccn.loc.gov/2018055821

10 9 8 7 6 5 4 3 2 1   19 20 21 22 23

Printed in China   62
This edition first printing, November 2019
Book design by Maria Mercado

CONTENTS

MEET THE CHARACTERS

Poppleton

Cherry Sue

Hudson

THE SHORE DAY

Poppleton was tired of
being landlocked.
He wanted to go to the shore.

"Hudson likes the shore,"
said Poppleton.
"I'll ask him to go, too."

Soon Poppleton and Hudson were on a bus, heading for the shore.

There were a lot of older ladies
on the bus.
They were a club.
They called themselves
"The Sassy Sues."

Hudson and Poppleton enjoyed
the ladies very much.

The ladies taught them new songs,
and new dances,
and how to win at poker.

When the bus got to the shore,
Hudson and Poppleton waved
good-bye to the ladies.

Poppleton had a big beach chair, which he unfolded.

Hudson had a little beach chair, which he unfolded.

They ate cheese sandwiches.
They watched the waves.
They collected shells.

At the end of the day,
they took the bus back home.

"Let's tell Cherry Sue about our day,"
said Poppleton.

Hudson and Poppleton went
to see Cherry Sue.

They gave her some shells
and a cheese sandwich.

They sang her some new songs.
They danced her some new dances.
They taught her how to win at poker.

They were very happy.
The shore day had been great.
But remembering it was even better.

DRY SKIN

Poppleton looked in the mirror
one morning.

"Yikes!" he cried.
"Dry skin!"

He looked closer.

"I am flaking away."

Poppleton called Cherry Sue.

"Cherry Sue," said Poppleton,
"I am as dry as an old apple.
What should I do?"

"Put on some oil," said Cherry Sue.

"All right," said Poppleton.

He put on some oil.

But the next day, the dry skin was back.

Poppleton called Cherry Sue again.

"I am as dry as a dandelion,"
said Poppleton.

"Did you put on some oil?"
asked Cherry Sue.

"It didn't help," said Poppleton.
"It just made me want french fries."

"Then put on some honey,"
said Cherry Sue.

"All right," said Poppleton.

He put on some honey.

But the next day, the dry skin was back.

Poppleton called Cherry Sue.

"I am as dry as a desert,"
said Poppleton.

"Did you put on some honey?"
asked Cherry Sue.

"It didn't help," said Poppleton.
"It just made me want biscuits."

"I'll be right over," said Cherry Sue.

When she walked into Poppleton's house,
Cherry Sue saw twenty empty french fry bags
and a chair full of crumbs.

"Told you," said Poppleton.

"Let me see your dry skin," said Cherry Sue.

Poppleton leaned over.

Cherry Sue looked closely.

"Poppleton, you don't have dry skin!"
said Cherry Sue.

"I don't?" asked Poppleton.

"You have **lint**!" said Cherry Sue.

"Lint?" asked Poppleton.
"Where did I get lint?"

"From that old sweater,"
said Cherry Sue.
"Poppleton, have you been wearing
the same linty sweater for three days?"
asked Cherry Sue.

Poppleton hung his head.
"I can be such a pig," he said.

"I'll be right back," said Cherry Sue.

Soon she came back with a lint brush.
"No llama can be without one," she said.

Poppleton brushed away the lint,
and threw away the bags,
and swept away the crumbs.

"I feel like a new pig,"
Poppleton said to Cherry Sue.

"You look like one," said Cherry Sue.
"Especially with that new wart
on your nose."

"WART?!!!" Poppleton screamed,
running for the mirror.

Cherry Sue giggled all the way home.

GRAPEFRUIT

One day Poppleton was watching TV.
The man on the TV said
grapefruit made people live longer.

Poppleton hated grapefruit.
But he wanted to live longer.
He wanted to live to be one hundred.

So he went to the store
and brought home some grapefruit.

59¢

He cut it up and took a little taste.
Poppleton's lips turned outside-in.

He took another little taste.
Poppleton's eyes made tears.

He took the tiniest taste
he could possibly take.
Poppleton's face turned green.

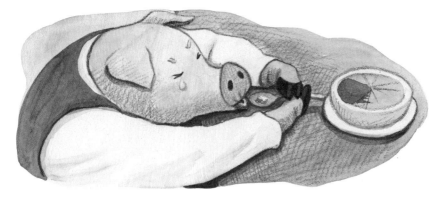

Poppleton's friend Hudson knocked at the door.

"Poppleton, why are you all green?" Hudson cried.
"And where are your lips?"

"I am eating grapefruit to live longer,"
said Poppleton.
"And it is making me sick."

"Then don't eat it!" cried Hudson.

"But I want to live to be one hundred,"
said Poppleton.

"With no lips?" asked Hudson.

"What else can I do?" asked Poppleton.

"Wait here," said Hudson.

Soon he was back with
a very, very, very old mouse.

"This is my Uncle Bill," said Hudson.
"Uncle Bill, tell Poppleton
how you lived to be one hundred."

Uncle Bill nodded.
He leaned over to Poppleton.

"Friends," he said.

"Friends?" asked Poppleton.

"Friends," said Uncle Bill.
"What did you do with your lips?"

When Uncle Bill and Hudson left,
Poppleton threw all of the grapefruit away.

And as soon as his lips came back,
he went out to find some friends.

ABOUT THE CREATORS

CYNTHIA RYLANT

has written more than one hundred books, including *Dog Heaven*, *Cat Heaven*, and the Newbery Medal–winning novel *Missing May*. She lives with her pets in Oregon.

MARK TEAGUE

lives in New York State with his family, which includes a dog and two cats, but no pigs, llamas, or goats, and only an occasional mouse. Mark is the author of many books and the illustrator of many more, including the How Do Dinosaurs series.

YOU CAN DRAW

 1. Draw a tall triangle.

 2. Add arms and legs. Keep it simple for now — you can always erase later!

 3. Draw a circle for Cherry Sue's head. The top of her head should meet the tip of the triangle. Add ears.

4. Give her eyes and a nose and a smile. Draw a "V" below her neck.

CHERRY SUE!

 5. Add detail to her arms and give the dress sleeves.

 6. Her tail and legs come next. Don't forget to add all of her hooves!

 7. Fill in details such as eyelashes and fur. That's Cherry Sue!

8. Color in your drawing!

WHAT'S YOUR STORY?

Poppleton and Hudson love riding the bus.
Have **you** ever taken a bus ride?
Where did you go?
Who did you meet?
Write and draw your story!